When her mother washes up dead in a creek after a solo kayak trip, Siri returns to her childhood summer house for a last visit.

She only intends to close up the house before leaving for good but some of the things she finds don't add up.

Were her mother's kayak trips only for fun, or were they part of something more sinister?

R.W. WALLACE

Author of the Ghost Detective Series

LIKE MOTHER LIKE DAUGHTER

A Mystery Short Story

Like Mother Like Daughter

by R.W. Wallace

Copyright © 2020 by R.W. Wallace

Copy editing by Jinxie Gervasio

Cover by the author

Cover Illustration 33024295 © andreykuzmin | 123rf.com

All characters and events in this book, other than those clearly in the public domain, are fictitious and any resemblance to real persons, living or dead, is purely coincidental.

All rights reserved. No part of this publication may be reproduced, distributed, or transmitted in any form or by any means, including photocopying, recording, or other electronic or mechanical methods, without the prior written permission of the publisher, except in the case of brief quotations embodied in critical reviews and certain other noncommercial uses permitted by copyright law. For permission requests, write to the publisher, addressed "Attention: Permissions Coordinator," at the address below.

www.rwwallace.com

ISBN: [979-10-95707-09-7]

Main category—Fiction

Other category—Mystery

First Edition

Also by R.W. Wallace

Mystery

The Tolosa Mystery Series
The Red Brick Haze (free)
The Red Brick Cellars
The Red Brick Basilica

Ghost Detective Shorts (coming soon)
Just Desserts
Lost Friends
Family Bonds
Till Death
Common Ground

Short Stories
Hidden Horrors
Cold Blue Eternity
Critters
Gertrude and the Trojan Horse
First Impressions
Let Them Eat Cake
Out of Sight
Two's Company
Like Mother Like Daughter

Science Fiction (short stories)

The Vanguard
Quarantine (Lollapalooza)
Common Enemies (Lollapalooza)

Adventure (short stories)

Size Matters

LIKE MOTHER
LIKE DAUGHTER

Georg and his fishing boat Måsen ease away from the dock at the speed of someone with a whole day of nothing ahead of them. The man has been a fixture in this community for as long as I can remember, but he doesn't have as much to occupy his time as he used to. His fishing boat's too small, he brings in too little fish and crabs to be profitable, the dock he worked with had to close because it couldn't compete with the larger docks in the larger cities… These days, he makes a living by taking German tourists out deep water fishing, and running a shuttle for people like me who don't have their own boats.

As I watch the fishing boat disappear behind an island, I ask myself for the millionth time what I'm doing here. *Here* being the mostly deserted island where my family has had its summer home for close to three decades, the one place that was a constant for me growing up.

The island's about one kilometer across from north to south (though the road going to the north has seen so little use over the past decade, it can hardly qualify as a path, and you need to know where it is to see it amongst the rapidly growing pines and heather), and perhaps two from east to west (not that anybody ever goes on foot to the westernmost point since it's nothing but bogs and mosquitoes). All fifteen or so houses (all summer houses; the island hasn't been inhabited year-round in over fifty years) are crammed on the southern and eastern shores, where they're the least exposed to the unforgiving wind coming in from the North Sea.

It's a harsh place, and its beauty sings to me in a way that no other place ever has. I never feel calmer than when I'm at the cairn on the island's culminating point (thirty-six meters above sea level, not exactly need for any climbing gear), the wind whipping through my hair and howling in my ears, and the waves of the Atlantic hitting the outer islands in huge, white explosions.

Right now, though—despite there being a decent wind bringing its salty taste in from the sea—I don't feel calm. I haven't since I learned of my mother's death. Can't seem to sit still.

My friend Clara claims I need "closure," but that doesn't sound like me. What's there to close?

I accepted the loss of my mother years ago. The fact that she's only now physically gone from this world doesn't really change anything. If anything, it should be a relief.

I don't think what I'm feeling is relief, though, but damned if I know what it is.

Shaking my head at my own stupid introspection, I shoulder my backpack and start the short trek up to our house. The large pines along the path have gained another meter in height since the last time I was here, and the neighbor's roses climb all the way to the second floor now. Other than that, everything's the same it's always been.

I shoulder the basement door open, wondering how much longer until it swells shut for good, and search for the spare key inside the broken floater in the back. The police had my mom's key, but I didn't feel like driving the three extra hours to retrieve it when I knew where the spare was.

The inside of the house looks like it always did, but something keeps me from going farther than just inside the door. I listen to the silence. Not even a fly buzzing. This place is so far away from civilization, every time I come I rediscover what silence really is. No cars in the distance, no planes or helicopters in the sky, no hooligans on scooters. No neighbors talking. The occasional boat will zoom by, but for the most part, it's a place for listening to your own thoughts.

I drop my bag on the floor and kick off my boots.

Everything looks normal. But the thing is, I know the police have been here, looking through everything for signs of anything out of the ordinary. I feel violated. Which makes no sense whatsoever since the only things I have here are some fifteen-year-old rags that I sometimes wear if I'm running out of clean clothes.

Shaking out of my funk, I step into the living room. On the floor, a pile of my mother's clothes greets me. I stare at it, thinking I should move them, but unwilling to actually do it.

She'd had an accident while out in her kayak. Since she'd been here alone, there would not have been any reason for her to tidy up her clothes for when she came back. The closer to the front door the better.

I'm somehow wondering if she would have preferred to be buried in these clothes, instead of the flowery dress I'd picked out from her closet at home. How would I know? I hardly knew the woman.

The silence becomes even more oppressing, reminding me of the numerous meals I'd shared with my mother without either of us ever saying a word. It was hardly ever an angry silence, mind, just…neutral.

That's my childhood. Neutral. No angry rows, and no gushing praise. Always in the middle. I often wondered if she noticed that I was there at all, or if she sometimes prepared food for two even when she was alone, thinking I was there.

I have no memory of my mother telling me she loved me.

According to my psychiatrist, she did, but didn't know how to show me. I'm not sure I believe her, but at least she helped me accept that that was just how my childhood had been and didn't have to influence my adult life.

I'd accepted the loss of my mother's love and moved on with my life.

In fact, I'd decided not to come here this year, and spend my vacation with friends, without feeling guilt about leaving my mother alone.

So much for that.

A knock sounds on the door, making me jump and hiss in a breath. "Hello?" a voice comes from outside.

"Coming," I say. A hand to my heart, I move to open the door.

A red-haired lady somewhere in her fifties gazes up at me from the front steps. "Hello," she repeats, somewhat haltingly. "I'm Nora, from the house just above the docks…" She's studying me, taking in my city clothing, my boots by the door, and the bag in the hallway. Then she lights up in a large grin. "You're Siri! Helga's daughter."

"Yes," I reply. I vaguely remember my mom talking about a Nora, but I have no idea who she is. A good friend of my mom's, or just an acquaintance? One of the people who basically grew up out here or one of the newcomers?

"I'm so happy to finally meet you," she gushes and comes up to shake my hand. "I'm usually working when you're here. But your mother has told me so much about you." Her sad smile wobbles.

"She did?" What did she say? She didn't know anything about my life.

"Of course," Nora says, oblivious to my disbelieving tone. "She was very proud of you. Loved to brag about how you speak four languages, and how you're working abroad."

Anyone with access to Facebook could find out that much about me.

Nora puts a hand on my shoulder. "She told me you did a parachute jump this year? That sounds so exciting!"

Okay. I certainly never told her about that. My mom may have stalked me on Facebook. I'm not sure how I feel about that fact.

She mistakes my hesitance for something else. "I'm so sorry for your loss," she says, excitement giving way to empathy. "I simply couldn't believe it when I received the news. The police were here asking questions and everything." She shakes her head and stares blindly at the cherry tree at the far end of the garden. "She went out in that kayak almost every day. She took that course on learning how to get back in if she ever fell out and everything." Her eyes snap back into focus. "I guess it just goes to show how precious life is. No matter how careful you are, an accident can happen quickly."

I nod, not knowing what to say. I'm never myself around my mother's friends, in case anything gets back to her and she gets ammunition to criticize me. Old habits die hard.

"I'm the one who called the Coast Guard," Nora offers. "Helga always told me where she was going and when to expect her back, so when the time she'd given me came and went, I called them." She shakes her head. "Took them almost two days to find her."

"Why was that?" I find myself asking. This place is really barren, and it shouldn't be that difficult to find a woman in a red wetsuit and her orange kayak.

Nora heaves an unhappy sigh. "The weather turned bad, for one. It had been just fine when your mother went out, but that night we got some very strong winds. They couldn't use the helicopter for an entire day. And she'd washed into a very secluded creek, with trees covering the line of sight from above, and seaweeds covered both her and her kayak."

The police had told me the same thing, but something just didn't ring true to me.

"How did she drown if she was so close to land?" I ask.

Nora squeezes my shoulder before letting go. "She probably fell in farther out and was washed in there during the storm.

Unfortunately, it's one of those situations where we'll probably never know for sure."

Also what the police had told me. And most likely the reason for my restlessness. How could they just say, "eh, we don't know, please get on with your life?"

"What happened to the kayak?" I ask, suddenly wondering if that's something else I need to retrieve from the police station.

Nora waves a hand toward the docks. "Oh, it's in the boathouse, in its usual spot. The police checked it, but didn't want to bring it with them, so I opened the boathouse for them. All her gear is there, too."

Oh. I hadn't expected that. Can't quite decide if I want to see the scene of the crime, so to speak.

"Well," Nora says and backs down the stairs. "Despite the circumstances, I'm thrilled to have finally made your acquaintance. Feel free to drop by while you're here, and we'll have a cup of coffee and some waffles."

I'm left alone with the silence.

By the next morning, I've concluded there are different types of silences, and the one I shared with my mother was not at all like the one filling the house right now. When there's somebody else in the house, but both parties choose to not speak, the silence is heavy, charged, full of unspoken words. When the silence is there because of somebody's absence, it's scarier, more profound. Final.

I turn on the radio and search for a station with minimum talk and maximum music. Whatever program I find seems to be on a nineties-roll, but that's okay. I'm not really listening.

I'd planned to go for a walk to the other side of the island this morning, but there's not even an inkling of a wind. The sea is blank like a plate of steel, reflecting the two picturesque clouds lazing around in the clear blue sky. It all looks very idyllic when the weather's like this, but I know better. This is when the tiny mosquitoes come out and eat you alive. Doesn't matter that they're no more than two millimeters from one wing tip to the other; if they're numerous enough, they'll win the battle against anyone.

The weather would be perfect for a trip in the kayak.

The thought pops into my head in my mother's voice, making a shiver run down my spine.

Though I'd accompanied her in a friend's kayak a number of times, going for an outing like that was really more my mother's thing than mine. There was no reason for me to go out now that she was no longer here.

In fact, I should probably sell the kayak. It would fetch a good price, seeing how well my mother took care of it.

I should probably check that nothing was broken.

And so, thirty minutes later, I find myself at the boathouse, wearing my usual too-big wetsuit (my mother's, which fit both of us better, is with the police, of course) and wondering at my sanity. Not that the mosquitoes let me wonder for long.

I drag the kayak down to the water, put on the skirt, and attach everything I find in the kayak to the elastic string criss-crossing the front. I'm not even sure what it's all for, but I seem to remember my mother saying it's mostly for getting back in the kayak if I ever end up in the water.

She, apparently, hadn't used any of it during her accident. Did that mean she'd been knocked unconscious before she even hit the water? If the storm had knocked her out of the kayak, it didn't really make sense that she'd used none of her emergency gear.

I wade a couple of steps into the water so the kayak no longer touches the rocky bottom, brace both hands on either side of the hole, step one foot inside…an promptly end up ass first in the water.

I'm in ten centimeters of water and I've managed to soak my entire wetsuit. Now that I think about it, it's possible my mother always told me to use the oar to stabilize the kayak while I got in.

The shock of the cold water quickly fades, the wetsuit doing its job. I place the oar in the water and hold onto it on top of the kayak, and with an abnormal amount of care, I manage to seat myself in the kayak.

I attach the skirt, close the clasp from the oar, bring down the keel, and wiggle my ass to find a comfortable position.

Five minutes later, I'm paddling full speed toward the east side of the island. I'd only intended to go for a short trip, just to check that none of the gear was broken, but now that I'm away from the mosquitoes and already wet, I figure I might as well get a decent trip in while I'm at it. The weather's gorgeous and if I sell the kayak, I may never get another opportunity like this.

I fall into the rowing routine; left side, right side, left side, right side. I feel my body remembering more and more of the technique, using my entire torso to glide along and not just my arms. I'll still be feeling it all over by tonight, but that's a worry for another time.

I encounter two families of ducks and feel fairly certain of spotting two different eagles. A shoal of mackerel makes the water boil only meters from my kayak, but I'm unable to actually see any of the fish. I meet very few jellyfish, two blue ones and one dangerous red—the warm weather this summer must not have agreed with them because the sea around here is usually teeming with the things.

The kayak touches a large rock in front of me as I approach a small creek. I've been so focused on the physical exercise and the wildlife around me, I've not really thought about where all this rowing took me.

Of course I've gone to the creek where my mother died.

Closure, here I come.

It looks so idyllic right now, with the sun reflecting in the still, blue waters, seagulls screaming overhead, and seaweed dancing below the water. In fact, I just might get out and go for a swim.

Or that might be too creepy. Aargh.

The kayak scrapes against those tiny white shell-thingies that cover all the rocks. I don't want to ruin the kayak, so I finally spring into action. My arms are getting seriously tired of rowing for over an hour, and my back hurts from sitting straight in an unfamiliar position.

A swim sounds like a perfect idea.

I once again roll around and end up in the water when I try to exit the kayak, but there's nobody but the seagulls to see me and in any case, I'm planning to go for a swim. So there.

I pull the kayak some way up the shore, so it won't take off without me. I grab my goggles where I'd stowed them in the pocket of the skirt and leave everything—including my cell phone in its protective bag—behind as I wade into the cold water.

With the wetsuit, the temperature is just perfect. I could stay here for hours without feeling cold.

Of course, I *would* get cold eventually. Could that be what happened to my mother? She ended up in the water and got so cold she suffered from hypothermia? Splashing around in the paradise-like creek, it's impossible to imagine.

But there was a storm.

Several hours *after* she was supposed to have returned home. She wasn't exactly in the habit of losing track of time. We were both physically incapable of being late for anything, our inner clock apparently the human version of a Swiss watch.

With a growl of frustration, I roll over on my stomach to get a view of the landscape below me in the waters. I've always loved doing this, watching the fish, the shrimp, the crabs, while floating above them like a benevolent god.

This spot is particularly nice because the rocky beach turns into sand about three meters in. It makes it so much easier to spot the crabs and the little fish, even an impatient toddler could do it. Still, I idle in place, lifting my head up to breathe when necessary, and enjoying the lulling sensation of the ocean around me.

A crab, abnormally large this close to shore, crosses an open patch of sand in its funny side-walking way. It looks odd, but it takes me a moment to realize why—both of its large claws are missing. The poor thing only has its six skinny stick legs left. How does it even manage to eat?

My attention is drawn to the sand moving below me—no, it's not sand, it's a flounder. The exact same beige and gray as the sand, with only its two black eyes allowing me to see where it settles half a meter farther away.

I smile to myself. Finally, a challenge. I search the sand, looking for more of the oddly shaped flat fish with both eyes on the same side of its head. Once I know what to look for, I see several. There's even a big one—if I'd had any sort of survival skill, I'd have tried to catch it because it'd make a delicious dinner—hiding close to some spaghetti-like seaweed.

Though I usually try not to bother the fish, I lower a foot toward the flounder to make it move.

It flees across the sand at lightning speed. My inner five-year-old is howling with glee.

A flash of light draws my eye. After going up for air, I focus on something dark where the flounder had just lain. When I move, sunlight reflects in whatever it is and blinks at me again.

Could someone have dumped a glass object in here? The local populace isn't always the best at preserving the nature around them, and too many consider the ocean as their private dumpster.

But this place is far from any habitation, and I'm not seeing any other litter.

It blinks at me again and my curiosity gets the best of me. A deep breath, and I try to swim down.

I say try, because the wetsuit is giving me extra buoyancy and I don't even manage to get my ass below water level. It's a good thing those seagulls won't be telling anyone about what they're seeing today.

I commit to actually needing to make an effort, and on the third try, I manage to swim down the two meters or so to the blinking object. I grab it and let myself float up and pop out of the water like some sort of children's bathroom toy.

It's a camera. I turn it over in my hands as I float on my back while regaining my breath. It looks familiar.

I gave a camera like this—water resistant down to fifteen meters or so—to my mother for her birthday a couple of years back.

Had there been a camera on the list of things the police had gathered from the creek and the kayak? I didn't think so. But then again, she didn't always bring the camera with her when she went kayaking—there's a limit to how many pictures of ocean, islands, and the tip of the kayak you need.

My finger hovers over the power button. My heart is hammering and it's no longer due to the effort of diving with a wetsuit.

The camera *could* have fallen out of the kayak or a pocket or something when my mother drowned.

Growling, I press the button. The screen flashes on—only to display a message saying the battery is flat and please recharge it.

Fine. I will.

I swim back to shore and get ready to paddle back home.

I SEARCH *EVERYWHERE* for the camera's charger. It's not in the living room (though I do find her computer), it's not in her room (the bed isn't made and for once in my life, my fingers itch to straighten everything out), and it's not in the kitchen (isn't that where everyone charges their electrical toys?). I'm tempted to check the toilet just for the hell of it, except it's an outhouse and doesn't have electricity.

Only when I give up, do I find it, hanging from that weirdo socket halfway up the wall in the living room. I've always said that my mother didn't have a sense of humor, but this gives me doubts. *Everybody* comments on that socket on the wall. What's it for? Was there a light at some point? Were they afraid the kids would stuff their fingers in?

My mother apparently finally found a use for it.

I pop in the camera's battery, then sit back, literally twiddling my thumbs. How long do I have to leave it to get enough juice to look at the pictures?

Wait.

I slap a hand to my forehead and lurch out of the couch to get the computer. I don't need the camera to look at the pictures.

There's a password, but my mother has used the same one for at least fifteen years. For once, I'm glad she didn't listen to me nagging her about internet security and net pirates.

Five minutes later, I'm opening the folder on the memory card, heart hammering and breath short. All this tension, and I'm going to find blurry pictures of crabs and seaweed.

First picture? A crab.

Huh.

Actually, it seems to be the same crab that I saw. The one with the missing claws.

I frown at the screen. Is that even possible?

I scroll to the next picture. Three more crabs. And none of them have their claws.

What's going on? Is this a newly evolved species of crab or something? But isn't evolution supposed to make things *better*? Why would it remove the crab's only way of defending itself, grabbing food, and bringing said food to its ridiculously small mouth?

The next picture is a little blurry because it's taken from farther away than the first two. But it's clear enough that I get the idea. The sea bottom is teeming with crabs, at least twenty or thirty.

And none of them have claws.

I squint at the top left corner. A clawless crab is *swimming* toward its buddies.

What?

Then the black spot at the top of the image makes sense, and so does everything else.

I scroll through the pictures until I find what I'm looking for. A clear shot of a fishing boat, the name—Måsen—easily recognizable, and the skipper's face visible beneath his battered cap. He's leaning over what I assume to be a crab trap while one hand throws a crab over board.

I'd be willing to bet my house on that crab having just been relieved of its claws.

My fists clench and I ground my teeth together as I sit there, all alone in the big house, angry at Georg for doing this to the poor creatures.

I'd heard talk of it some time back. That some official-sounding group went out and said that we couldn't eat the meat in the crab's shell because of some algae or something, that only the claws were fit for human consumption. A couple of fishermen had tried to keep fishing the crabs, but only keeping the claws to sell.

Unsurprisingly, lots of people and several animal rights groups went crazy angry at this, and crab fishing was banned during the period where the body wasn't edible.

So why was Georg still doing it?

And why was my mother taking pictures?

I spend hours in front of my mother's computer that night, zooming in on all the pictures, taking in every little detail. I *think* the pictures were taken not far from the creek where I was today—the one where my mother was found dead—but it's honestly difficult to tell one anemone-covered rock from another.

I also go through her older pictures and find several similar shots, though it seems like that last time was the only occasion where she caught the fisherman on camera actually mangling the crabs. She had several sessions where she took pictures of the poor crabs on the sea floor, and a couple of Georg at the dock handing over a bag full of something to that week's German tourists. Presumably selling the claws, but it's not explicit in the pictures.

When I go to bed, my head is spinning. There's absolutely no proof that there's any connection between Georg making hundreds of crabs die a slow, agonizing death, and my mother's passing. But it does smell suspicious.

The next morning, I'm not feeling any wiser, but a good night's sleep gives me the energy to want to search further.

And I want to get off the island. I don't know if it's closure, but I don't feel the need to be here anymore. In fact, I think I need to be somewhere else.

I call and arrange for Georg to pick me up in an hour—because he's still my only means of transportation around here—and pack my things.

With a last glance at the worn-down house and a silent farewell to my memories here with my mother, I go to the docks to wait for Georg the crab-torturer.

Standing on the docks, I'm sweating and my head's spinning. I regret dressing the way I did, but it seemed like a good idea at the time and it's too late to change now. I'd claim momentary insanity, except it seems to be permanent.

I watch as the fishing boat crosses the body of water between the mainland and my little island.

Like so many locals, Georg hasn't always shown the greatest respect for the environment he lives in. For example, his boathouse is filled to the rim with junk, but Georg doesn't even see it. He's not here to make pretty, picturesque boathouses, he's here to fish. Still, I can't wrap my mind around him ripping the claws off hundreds of crabs to sell them for a pretty penny to his precious Germans. They probably don't even know it's illegal to fish the crabs, so why would they question their host for selling them?

Måsen eases in along the docks and Georg greets me in his usual, half-sour half-timid expression and grunt.

I heave my stuff on board and off we go.

My mother was always really good at finding things to discuss with Georg during the fifteen-minute trip to the mainland, but I'd never known what to say to the man.

"When was the last time you saw my mother?" I blurt out, before pinching my lips shut in embarrassment.

Georg doesn't seem to find it odd. "Helped the police ferry her kayak back," he says with his usual lack of expression, like bringing a dead woman's kayak home was something he did every day.

"Right." I swallow. "And before that?"

He sucks on his lip for a moment. "Saw her out in her kayak from time to time."

"Did you know she took pictures of you?" I've lost all control of what comes out of my mouth. At some level, I still don't believe this man is cruel, and I'm hoping he'll be able to explain all the pictures.

This time I get a reaction. Georg takes his eyes off the water (it's not like there's anything to see—we're going straight ahead across an empty patch of water for fifteen minutes and there's just one other boat in view) and stares at me. "Pictures?"

"Of you fishing crabs." I wait for a beat. "Lots of times."

He chews on his lip some more. "My family needs food," he says.

"So that who's eating all the crab claws?" Even I don't know if I could actually believe that or if I'm just playing dumb.

"Ain't no business but my own what I do on my boat." He glances ahead to check our course. Even during a discussion like this he's hard-wired to take care of his boat first, everything else second.

"There are rules, though," I say. "And those poor crabs…" I pull out the camera and show him the picture of the twenty clawless crabs erring on the sand below his boat.

Georg grabs the camera and throws it overboard.

Okay. It might be able to take pictures below water, but there's no way I'm getting it back from the eighty-meter deep ocean below us.

"The pictures are backed up on the cloud," I say absently. Accepting that I've lost all control of what I'm saying, I ask, "Did you kill my mother because she was going to turn you in?"

There's finally real anger showing in Georg's blue eyes. I've known him for thirty years and I've only ever seen him with the same bland expression. Now his nostrils are flaring and red blotches appear high on his cheeks.

"She was meddling with stuff that wasn't her business," he says. And gives me a shove.

I give a surprised shriek as I stumble backwards. My back hits the railing, but it's too low and I have too much momentum. I topple over, going head first into the water.

When I resurface a moment later, the fishing boat is already a good twenty meters away from me. Georg doesn't spare me as much as a glance—his eyes are back on where his precious boat is headed.

Now what?

The cool water seems to improve my brain capacity somewhat. I realize that despite the overheating, I was right to wear the wetsuit below my rain jacket. I pretty much float without effort, and I'm nowhere close to cold.

I kick off my sneakers and watch them float up beside me. How come they drag me down, but on their own they float?

As I lay back to settle in for a long swim, I hear voices.

It's the boat I'd spotted earlier and it's coming to save me.

Turns out the entire family on that little boat had seen Georg shove me into the water. They brought me back to shore (while giving me the side-eye for wearing a wetsuit *and* normal clothing) and helped me call the police.

I never saw my backpack again. I didn't even bother asking the police to ask Georg what he'd done with it. I assume he dumped it in the ocean, since that seemed to be his go-to solution.

The important part: the police managed to get a confession out of Georg after pretending that my mother had photographed a lot more than him killing crabs.

Faced with my mother knowing of his crab-fishing crimes, he'd chosen to kill her. Like most fishermen, he couldn't swim, but he knew his way around a fishing boat. He'd thrown a fishing net over her so she'd get entangled, then used a pole to make her fall into the water.

The net stopped her from being able to get out of the kayak, or to right herself with her oar.

Once she was dead, Georg had untangled her from the net and dragged her and her body into the nearby creek.

I wouldn't have expected that learning that my mother had been murdered would be a relief, but this time I recognized the feeling. And there was some pride, too.

She'd apparently rowed right up to his boat and confronted him with her accusations. Shortsighted and impulsive.

Like mother like daughter.

THANK YOU

THANK YOU FOR reading *Like Mother Like Daughter!* I hope you enjoyed the story.

Without any big surprise, the inspiration for this story came during a kayaking trip—with my mother. While she admired the eagles, ducks, and anemonies, I plotted murder...

If you liked the the story, you might want to check out some of my other books mentioned on the next page. It's mostly Mysteries, but a few Science Fiction short stories will pop up, too.

And don't forget that the first book of my *Tolosa Mystery* series, *The Red Brick Haze*, is available for free on my website.

R.W. Wallace
www.rwwallace.com

Also by R.W. Wallace

Mystery

The Tolosa Mystery Series
The Red Brick Haze (free)
The Red Brick Cellars
The Red Brick Basilica

Ghost Detective Shorts (coming soon)
Just Desserts
Lost Friends
Family Bonds
Till Death
Family History
Common Ground
Heritage
Eternal Bond
New Beginnings

Short Stories
Cold Blue Eternity
Hidden Horrors
Critters
Gertrude and the Trojan Horse
First Impressions
Let Them Eat Cake
Out of Sight
Two's Company
Like Mother Like Daughter

Fantasy (Short Stories)
Unexpected Consequences
Morbier Impossible
A Second Chance

Science Fiction (Short Stories)
The Vanguard

Lollapalooza Shorts
Quarantine
Common Enemies
Coiled Danger
Mars Meeting

Adventure (Short Stories)
Size Matters

www.ingramcontent.com/pod-product-compliance
Lightning Source LLC
LaVergne TN
LVHW041717060526
838201LV00043B/783